For Sam, Ben, Nick
Alex, Logan and Jennifer

Also published by Ruwanga Trading:

The Whale Who Wanted to be Small
The Wonderful Journey
The Gift of Aloha
The Shark Who Learned a Lesson
Gecko Hide and Seek
The Goodnight Gecko
The Brave Little Turtle
Tikki Turtle's Quest
Happy as a Dolphin, *A Child's Celebration of Hawai'i*
How the Geckos Learned to Chirp

First published 1988 by Ruwanga Trading
ISBN 978-0961510244
Printed in China by Everbest Printing Co., Ltd

BOOK ENQUIRIES AND ORDERS:
Booklines Hawaii, a division of The Islander Group
269 Pali'i Street
Mililani, Hawaii 96789
Phone: 808-676-0116, ext.206
Fax: 808-676-5156
Toll Free: 1-877-828-4852
Website: www.islandergroup.com

A Whale's Tale

written and illustrated by
Gill McBarnet

Ruwanga  Trading

One day Kanani the baby whale and her grandmother Tutu Whale, visited their friends in the sunlit reefs of Hawaii. Leilani Anemone and her sisters were doing a hula, their arms moving gracefully with every swell and sigh of the ocean. Tako Octopus played his ukelele and all the sea creatures swayed in time to the music.

Suddenly all the sea creatures scattered. Koko Crab was up to another of his tricks. With one of his claws he had grabbed a parrotfish by the tail, and the angry fish spun round and round. . .

. . .until she finally

. . .shook him off.

The little crab scuttled under a rock and peeped out at them, his eyes twinkling with mischief. Tutu chuckled and said to Kanani "That reminds me of the time a crab grabbed Willie the whale by the tail. . ."
"Tell us the story Tutu, *please!*" begged Kanani.

Kanani and her friends gathered around.
"Well. Willie Whale spun around until the little crab let go. He was a young whale and had never really noticed his tail before, but after that he saw that it followed him wherever he went. It wiggled merrily through the water and he just *had* to catch it, so he began chasing his tail. Faster and faster he spun, but no matter how fast he swam, he wasn't *quite* able to catch it. The other sea creatures were astonished. They had never known a whale who chased his tail."

Then Tutu Whale continued her tale. . .

There was a young whale called Willie
who everyone thought was so silly.
The reason you see
is that Willie took glee
In chasing his tail merrily.

"We think you're absurd,
       because we've never heard
Of a whale who chases his tail."
       But Willie just smiled
And never got riled
       as he followed his tail willy-nilly.

Cecilia the eel
    said with a squeal
"A tail-chasing whale
    isn't right or genteel.
We'll not be your friends,
    then see how you feel."

"I also appeal"
said Sammy the seal.
"You're a whale, not a wheel
so stop this ordeal.
Stop it now Willie,
and don't be so silly."

Said Myrtle the turtle
        "Why do you hurtle,
Chasing your tail with your head?
        If you want to circle,
You'll make me turn-turtle
        and hurtle with turtles instead."

"May I say," said a ray
        "Here's a fun way to play!
Why don't you sway
        with your tail in this way.
I say, can you sway?"

*"Sway or swish," cried the fish
"We all wish you would learn
That we think it is foolish
just to turn turn turn."*

"A tail is for swishing,
swish swish swish.
How we wish you would swish
as we little fish wish."

But Willie the whale still chased his tail,
    spinning ever faster.
Until a very near disaster
    brought him to a sudden STOP.

With a great flip flop,
    Willie the whale
Bumped into his Pop.

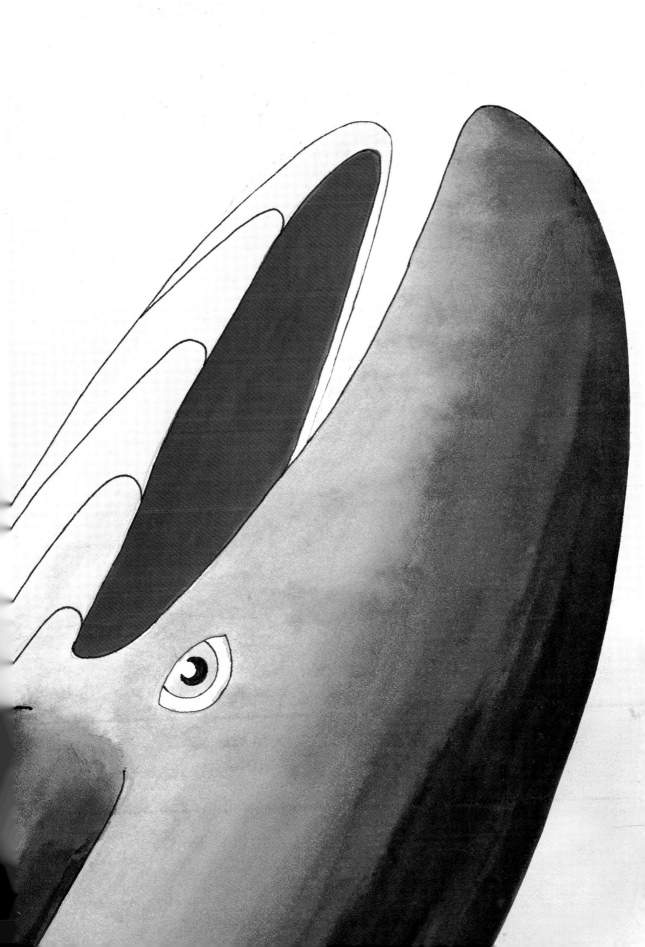

"Hello Willie, Hi my son.
   I can see you're having fun,
As round your tail you've spun and spun.

But as a whale you need to know
   there's more to tails than spinning so.
While Danno Dolphin plays his uke,
   I'll show you how I use my fluke*."

* The two "wings" on the end of a whale's tail are called the fluke.

"Flukes are fun and here's one way
    your Poppa Whale can sway his tail.

Above the water watch me flap it.
Watch me wave
    and slip slap, slap it."

"When deep down I want to dive,
I flap my fluke
and
down
I
glide."

*"Here's one your friends
the little fish
Would call a giant tailswish."*

"Lazily on my side I lie
Then. . .
swish swish
Watch those bubbles fly!"

"Our tails are long
        and very strong
So when we jump to the sky
        our tails can push us really high."

*"We cannot fly
      but we can breach*,
I will teach —
      then you can try."*

* A "breach" is when a whale leaps out of the water.

"However...

Should you anger any whale,
    keep clear of his thrashing tail.
Whales are peaceful, as you know,
    but they can strike a mighty blow."

"But tails are helpful
tails I love,
Below the water or above.

We're born with tails
and it's our fate
That with our tails
we whales are great!"

Then "HOORAY, HOORAY!"
cheered his friends that day. . .

. . .as Willie the whale
waved his tail.

"What a great tale!" said Kanani Whale
as they swam away
on that sunny day.